2-99

CR V

The Bookworm's Feast

A POTLUCK OF POEMS

J. Patrick Lewis

pictures by John O'Brien

3 1336 04891 4767

Dial Books for Young Readers New York

CHILDREN'S SERVICES
SAN DIEGO PUBLIC LIBRARY

THE GENTLEMAN BOOKWORM

There once was a Gentleman Bookworm
Ate his words with a fork and a spoon.
    When friends crawled down
    From Book End Town,
He offered them *Goodnight, Moon*.

He fed them *The Wind in the Willows*
And a page out of *Charlotte's Web*.
    They were eating bizarre
    Where the Wild Things Are,
When one of the guestworms said,

"How sinfully rich and delicious!
Why should anyone bother to cook?
    You've done it, dear boy!
    Now sit down and enjoy
A bite of this poetry book!"

Having dined on the Table of Contents,
A worm, wiggling up to the host,
    Said, "When do we eat?"
    "Ah, *bon appétit!*"
Cried the Gentleman Bookworm. "A toast!

"Here's a bowl of my favorite verses
And a dish of ridiculous rhyme!
    But might I suggest ...?"
    Said the host to the guest,
"Chew them slowly. One line at a time!"

So the worm waved her postage-stamp napkin.
Curled up in a little round ball,
    She proceeded to swallow
    The poems that follow
Until she had swallowed them all.

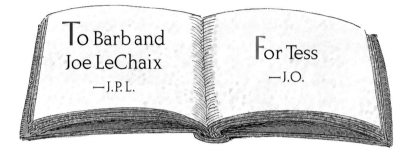

To Barb and
Joe LeChaix
—J. P. L.

For Tess
—J.O.

Published by Dial Books for Young Readers
A member of Penguin Putnam Inc.
375 Hudson Street
New York, New York 10014

Text copyright © 1999 by J. Patrick Lewis
Pictures copyright © 1999 by John O'Brien
All rights reserved
Designed by Julie Rauer
Printed in Hong Kong
First Edition
1 3 5 7 9 10 8 6 4 2

Library of Congress Cataloging in Publication Data
Lewis, J. Patrick.
The bookworm's feast: a potluck of poems/ J. Patrick Lewis;
pictures by John O'Brien.—1st ed.
p. cm.
Summary: A collection of poems on a variety of topics,
organized according to the courses of a meal.
ISBN 0-8037-1692-3.—ISBN 0-8037-1693-1 (lib. bdg.)
1. Children's poetry, American. [1. American poetry.]
I. O'Brien, John, date, ill. II. Title.
PS3562.E9465B66 1999   811'.54—dc20   94-31897   CIP   AC

The artwork for this book was created using black ink,
concentrated watercolors, and assorted dyes.

Appetizers

HEAVY METAL FELLOW

CLIPPER SHIP

HUNKY-DUNKY DONKEY

THE HIPPOPOTAMOLE

PIGEONS

HEAVY METAL FELLOW

Milo Armadillo,
Heavy metal fellow,
Lives beside a hollow
West of Amarillo.

Though he'll seldom follow
Fellows up a hill-o,
Milo likes to wallow
Underneath a willow.

If you holler, "HELLO,
MILO ARMADILLO!"
Don't expect a bellow—
Milo's rather mellow.

CLIPPER SHIP

Cries a sheep to a ship on the Amazon
(A clipper sheep ship that her lamb is on),
"Remember, dear Willy,
The nights will be chilly,
So keep your white woolly pajamazon!"

HUNKY-DUNKY DONKEY

There
was a
monkey,
Spanky,
who met
a donkey,
Dinky.
They
had a
funky
hunky-
dory
story
sort of
life,

Because
the
monkey,
Spanky,
had asked
the donkey,
Dinky,
if she
would
be his
hunky-
dunky
donkey
sort of
wife.

THE HIPPOPOTAMOLE

Whenever Hippopotamole
    Goes digging underground,
He noses up a load of coal
    By pushing dirt around.

So if the earth begins to shake,
    Don't get the hot and cold chills.
The Hippopotamole's just mak-
    Ing mountains out of molehills.

PIGEONS

Of all the birds in America,
  It isn't any wonder
Why Pigeons are the expert birds
  You never should stand under.

Sherbets

THE TABLESPOON GALLOPS AWAY

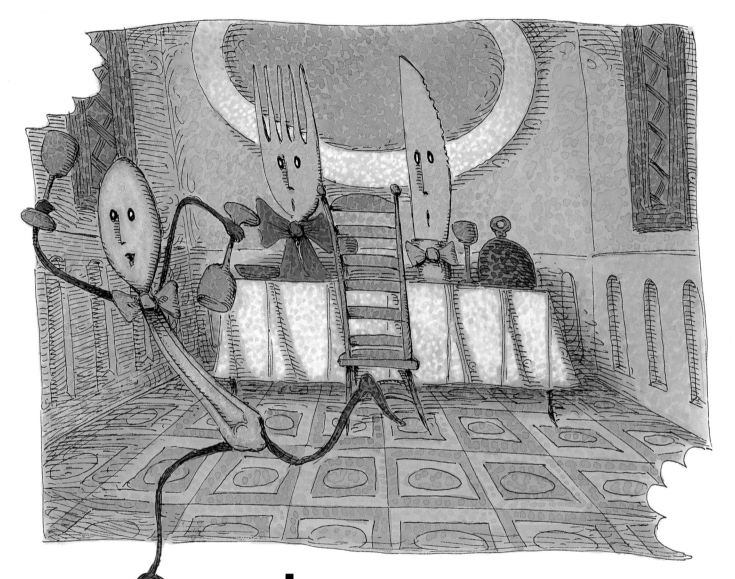

In Oneida, New York,
Live a Knife and a Fork
And a pip of a Tablespoon.

Whenever he passes
The Waterford glasses,
The Tablespoon tinkles a tune.

Knife and Fork sit at supper
With beautiful Tupper-
Ware bowls full of spinach soufflé,

While the Tablespoon gallops
Around with the scallops,
And cries, "Hi-ho, Silver! Away!"

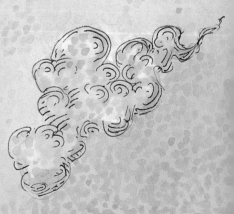

ORANGE JOHNSON

Orange Johnson
　　Wakes at dawn,
Puts his golden
　　Slippers on,
Climbs the summer
　　Sky at noon,
Trading places
　　With the moon.

Orange Johnson
　　Runs away
With the blue tag
　　End of day,
Switching off the
　　Globe lamplight,
Pulling down the
　　Shades of night.

HER-I-CANE

There was a curly her-i-cane,
Her name was Lorelei,
And all she ever wanted was
    To fly, fly, fly.

She wasn't like the other girls,
For Lori never grew
Into a proper her-i-cane
    That flew, flew, flew.

She twisted 'round the ocean.
She meant to touch the sky.
It took her tiny breath away
    To try, try, try.

So Lorelei decided
To a gentle wind be true—
She breezed right into autumn
    And she blew, blew, blew.

Entrees

THE FRAMBOISE FAIR

Mother, Mother, what shall I wear?
I've no new dress for the Framboise Fair.

Daughter, Daughter, I'll spin you one,
Spin it and spin it until it's spun.

Mother, Mother, how can I dance
A jig with the jigalong boy from France?

Daughter, Daughter, I'll cobble a pair
Of dancing slippers for you to wear.

Mother, Mother, look how it shows!
How can I possibly powder my nose?

Daughter, Daughter, open a sack
Of baking soda, and give it a whack!

Mother, Mother, shouldn't I take
A French Silk pie or a Hurry-Up cake?

Daughter, Daughter, there on the shelf,
Sift the flour, and bake it yourself!

PAULIE McCOY

Paulie McCoy, Paulie McCoy,
A peanut buttery bit of a boy,
Ate one peanut buttery cup—
Peanut Paulie grew up, up, up!
Ate two slices of raisin toast—
Raised him taller than a telephone post.
Ate three dreamsicles, by and by,
Paulie grew twenty-two stories high.
Ate four double-dark chocolate bars…
Paulie McCoy is seeing stars.

WHAT TO WEAR WHERE

When I was a boy
In Looziana,
We wore blue jeans
And a red bandanna.

Folks moved up
To the state of Maine,
We wore duck shoes
In slicker-suit rain.

Folks moved down
To the state of Texas,
We wore brand names,
Like Lazy X's.

Now that we're living
It up in Vermont,
We wear pretty much
Whatever we want.

BENNY SAID, RUBY SAID

Benny said
To Ruby Lee,

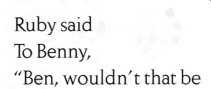
"M-A-R-R-Y M-E!"

Ruby said
To Benny,
"Ben, wouldn't that be

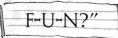
F-U-N?"

Benny said,
"My Ruby Lee,
We will W-E-D
Only if you let me K-
I-S-S you
Every day!"

HOME SWEET HOME

I met my wife in Houdy, Miss.
　　Or was it Odear, Me.?
We bought a house in Fiven, Tenn.
　　And lived so happily.

But then we moved to Shapeless, Mass.,
　　From there to Reeley, Ill.
And ended up in Sayno, Mo.,
　　Where folks keep mighty still.

PROMISES, PROMISES

I married a man on Sunday.
He said, *"My dear, I do*

Love washing clothes on Monday,
I'll wash them just for you!

I'll iron them on Tuesday
If you will let me scrub

The floors, and twice on Wednesday,
The rings around the tub.

Oh, feather-dusting Thursday
Is work I won't ignore,

Because, my darling, Friday's
My day at the grocery store!"

His promises on Saturday
Rained down as thick as hail—

Which brings me back to Sunday—
So ends this fairy tale!

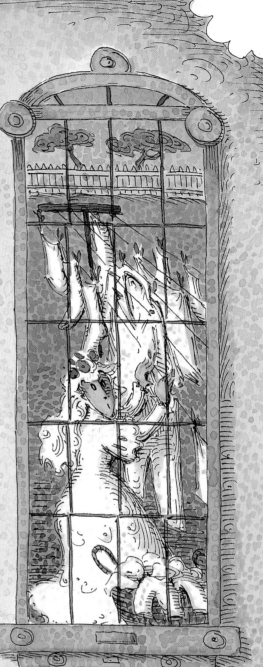

Sumptuous Side Dishes

TOE-COUNTING RHYME

RED RADISH, GREEN GARNISH

GREEN WILLY

SAY, HAY, WON'T YOU BE MINE?

TOE-COUNTING RHYME

Idaho pota-*toe,*
Ital-i-an toma-*toe,*
Banana, oh Chiqui-*toe!*
Where is my Pepi-*toe?*
Who's this hiding in the grass?
Must be some Mosqui-*toe!*

Bzzz, bzzz, bzzz

RED RADISH, GREEN GARNISH

So reddish
the radish
that grows
in my garden.

So greenish
the garnish
that graces
my plate.

So tannish
the tater
that tickles
my butter.

So hurry
please hurry
my dinner
is late.

GREEN WILLY

An Onion named Willy ran off to the ocean,
Rented a raft from a Carrot named Dick,
Set out to sea but the rocking-chair motion
Turned him as green as a Celery stick.

Green Willy, Green Willy, Green Willy, they called him,
Bobbing along on the Vegetable Seas.
Cucumber green was the sail that hauled him
Off to the Island of Broccoli Trees.

SAY, HAY, WON'T YOU BE MINE?

If you were the last brown bale of hay
And I were a melon vine,
I might just creep on up to you—
    Say, hay, won't you be mine?

If you were a husk of Indian corn
And I were a bolder crow,
We'd wait for Grandma Frost to dust
    This meadow white with snow.

If you were a thousand columbines
And I were your long cool drink,
A charm of hummingbirds could spend
    All summer here, I think.

Delectable Desserts

THE ALPHABET GANG

A was an Actor in comedy parts
B was a Baker of raspberry tarts
C was a Carpenter hammering wood
D was a Doctor who did what he could
E was an Expert at taste-testing tea
F was a Fool, who said, "Who follows me?
      *Some*one must follow me, good golly ... Gee!"

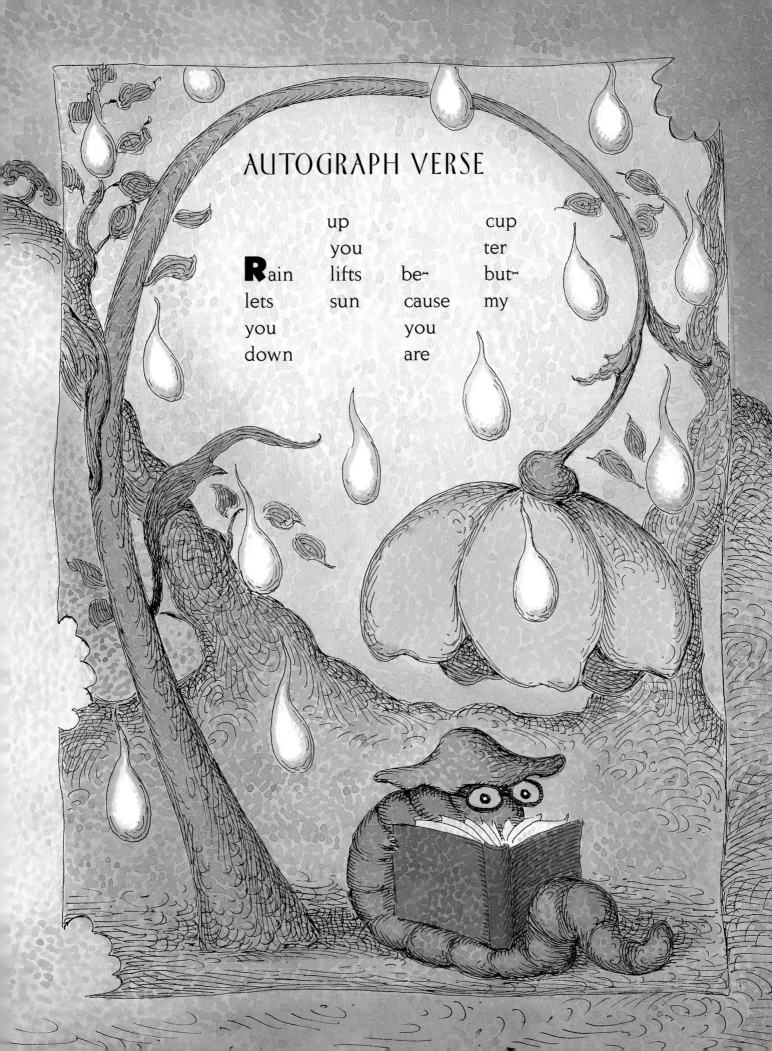

AUTOGRAPH VERSE

Rain lets you down

up you lifts sun

be- cause you are

cup ter but- my

READ...THINK...DREAM

Book me a passage
 to history
Back to some once-
 on-a-time,
Sail me into a
 tall told tale,
Read me a river-
 boat rhyme.

Ride me the waves
 of a story,
Settle me down
 by a brook,
Dream me a land
 only dreamed of,
Book me a voyage
 by book.

POSTCARD POEM

PLACE
STAMP
HERE

Find yourself a quarter
Buy yourself a stamp
Tap it on your tongue
Until it's damp damp damp
Stick it on a postcard
Mail it to a friend
Tell her you will be one
Till the end end end!

TWO GOOD BOOKS

If you were a book,
What book would you be?
Alice in Wonderland?
Life in the Sea?

    If I were a book,
    I'd be *Rumpelstiltskin,*
    'Twas the Night Before Christmas,
    Or *Huckleberry Finn.*

If we were two blockbuster
Books on the shelves,
We'd tingle our spines
Reading us to ourselves....

    Then we'd do the same thing
    All the other books did—
    We'd wait to be borrowed
    By some lucky kid.

THE END OF THE BOOKWORM'S FEAST

So the Gentleman's Potluck had ended,
Not a poem-crumb littered the floor.
    When the worms who were able
    Crawled down from the table,
The host met his guests at the door.

"Now remember," he said as they wiggled
Home to book nooks and paperback racks,
    "It's especially wise
    To combine exercise
With a bowlful of poetry snacks!"

"Oh, what fun!" cried the gaggle of guestworms,
Who were laughing so hard that they shook.
    Then the giggling gourmet
    Up and wiggled away...

And dove into a poetry book!

Thanks to the following bookworms in whose pages these poems first appeared or are forthcoming:

Caroline Feller Bauer, "There Once Was a Gentleman Bookworm" in *The Poetry Break* (H.W. Wilson).
Ranger Rick: "Heavy Metal Fellow."
Myra Cohn Livingston, "Clipper Ship" in *Lots of Limericks* (Simon and Schuster).
Spider: "Hunky-dunky Donkey."
Lee Bennett Hopkins, "Orange Johnson" in *Weather* (HarperCollins).
Light Quarterly: "Home Sweet Home."
Ladybug: "The Alphabet Gang."
The Children's Book Council: "Read...Think...Dream."

THE END OF THE BOOKWORM'S FEAST

So the Gentleman's Potluck had ended,
Not a poem-crumb littered the floor.
    When the worms who were able
    Crawled down from the table,
The host met his guests at the door.

"Now remember," he said as they wiggled
Home to book nooks and paperback racks,
    "It's especially wise
    To combine exercise
With a bowlful of poetry snacks!"

"Oh, what fun!" cried the gaggle of guestworms,
Who were laughing so hard that they shook.
    Then the giggling gourmet
    Up and wiggled away...

And dove into a poetry book!

Thanks to the following bookworms in whose pages these poems first appeared or are forthcoming:

Caroline Feller Bauer, "There Once Was a Gentleman Bookworm" in *The Poetry Break* (H.W. Wilson).
Ranger Rick: "Heavy Metal Fellow."
Myra Cohn Livingston, "Clipper Ship" in *Lots of Limericks* (Simon and Schuster).
Spider: "Hunky-dunky Donkey."
Lee Bennett Hopkins, "Orange Johnson" in *Weather* (HarperCollins).
Light Quarterly: "Home Sweet Home."
Ladybug: "The Alphabet Gang."
The Children's Book Council: "Read...Think...Dream."